LAUNDRY DAY

Jessixa Bagley

A NEAL PORTER BOOK
ROARING BROOK PRESS
NEW YORK

For Baxter who has the most
(but cutest) laundry of all

Copyright © 2017 by Jessixa Bagley

A Neal Porter Book

Published by Roaring Brook Press

Roaring Brook Press is a division of Holtzbrinck Publishing Holdings Limited Partnership

175 Fifth Avenue, New York, New York 10010

The art for this book was created with pen and watercolor on paper.

mackids.com

Library of Congress Cataloging-in-Publication Data

Names: Bagley, Jessixa, author.

Title: Laundry day / Jessixa Bagley.

Description: First edition. | New York : Roaring Brook Press, 2017. | "A Neal
Porter book." | Summary: "Two bored badgers have run out of things to do
until their mom suggests they help with the laundry"— Provided by
publisher.

Identifiers: LCCN 2016002012 | ISBN 9781626723177 (hardback)

Subjects: | CYAC: Badgers—Fiction. | Laundry—Fiction. | House
cleaning—Fiction. | BISAC: JUVENILE FICTION / Social Issues / Friendship.
| JUVENILE FICTION / Humorous Stories. | JUVENILE FICTION / Imagination &
Play.

Classification: LCC PZ7.1.B3 Lau 2017 | DDC [E]—dc23

LC record available at https://lccn.loc.gov/2016002012

Our books may be purchased in bulk for promotional, educational, or business use. Please
contact your local bookseller or the Macmillan Corporate and Premium Sales Department
at (800) 221-7945 ext. 5442 or by e-mail at MacmillanSpecialMarkets@macmillan.com.

First edition 2017   Book design by Jennifer Browne

Printed in China by RR Donnelley Asia Printing

Solutions Ltd., Dongguan City, Guangdong Province

1 3 5 7 9 10 8 6 4 2

"I'm bored," said Tic.

"Me too," said Tac.

"Why don't you two read a book?
You love to read," said Ma Badger.
"We read all our books," said Tic.
"Then we read them backward," said Tac.

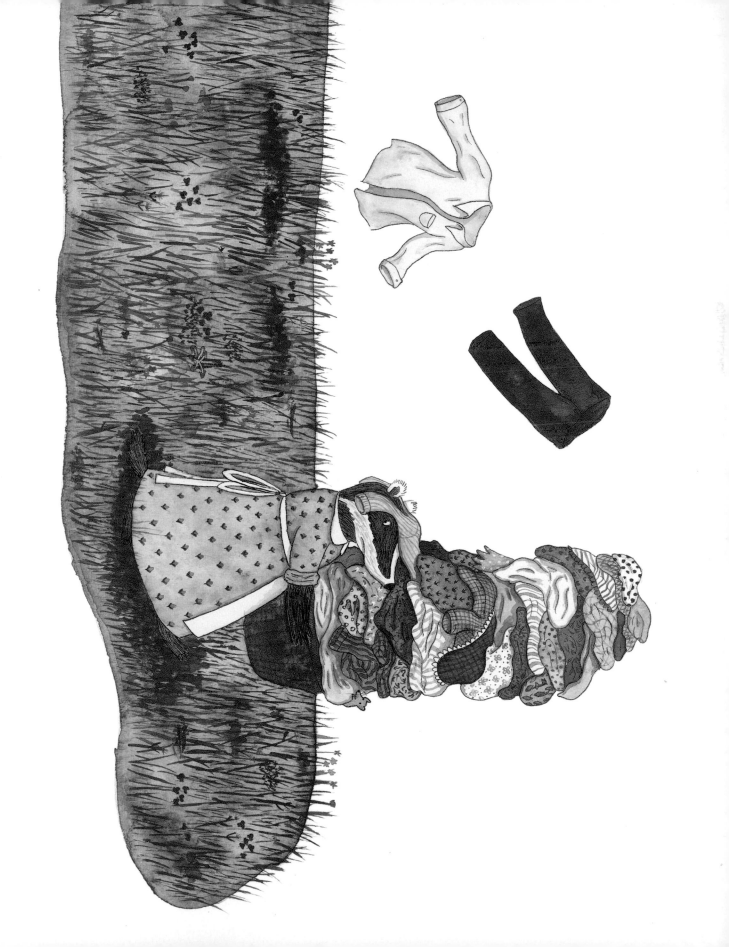

"Well, how about building a fort?" asked Ma Badger.

"We already made one," said Tic.

"Then we invaded it, and it fell apart," said Tac.

"What about fishing?" asked Ma Badger tiredly.

"We caught all of the fish in the pond," said Tac.

"Then we let them go," said Tic.

"Well, would you like to help me hang the laundry?" said Ma Badger.

"Laundry?" Tic asked, looking surprised.

"We haven't done that yet," said Tac.

"Okay!" they chimed together.

"Let me show you how. Take the wet clothes and sheets out of the basket. Don't let them fall on the ground. Then take the clothespins and clip them on the line."

"Like this?" asked Tic.

"Very good!" said Ma Badger.

"It's so easy!" shouted Tac from the other end of the clothesline.

"Will you boys finish hanging the laundry for me while I go to the market?" asked Ma Badger.

"Sure, Ma!" chirped Tic and Tac.

Tic and Tac quickly went to work hanging every shirt, sock, sheet, and sweater that was in the basket.

"That was fun! But we're out of laundry already," said Tic.

"Hmm . . . I have an idea!" said Tac.

"We can hang the winter clothes and blankets!" said Tac.

"Good thinking!" said Tic.

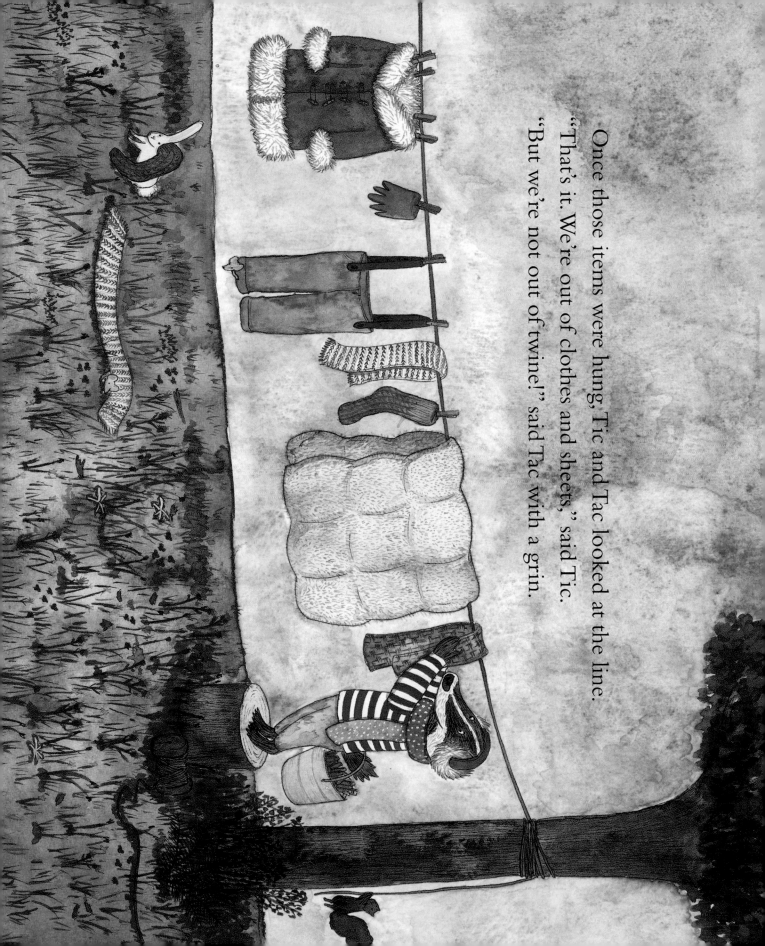

Once those items were hung, Tic and Tac looked at the line.

"That's it. We're out of clothes and sheets," said Tic.

"But we're not out of twine!" said Tac with a grin.

Tic and Tac ran inside and each grabbed an apple barrel full of odds and ends from the house and started to hang them up.

"This is great!" shouted Tic.

"It sure is! What else
is there?!" asked Tac.

They ran all over the house gathering every whatnot, bauble, and trinket they could find! They picked up every knickknack, this and that, and bric-a-brac in the house. They grabbed buckets and books.

They pilfered the pots.

They pirated pillows.

They looted lampshades and even took the toaster!

They hung everything they could
find that wasn't nailed down.

"We're really good at this!" said Tic proudly.

"I'm pretty impressed myself!" said Tac.

But just then . . .
Ma came home from the market.

"TIC AND TAC! What have you done?!"
she hollered.

"Um, we hung up the laundry?" said Tic.

"Uh . . . and a few other things," said Tac.

"Well, I'm not sure how you did it,"
said Ma Badger.
"But you forgot a couple of things."

"I'm bored," said Tic.

"Me too," said Tac.

"I wonder if Ma needs help with dinner!"